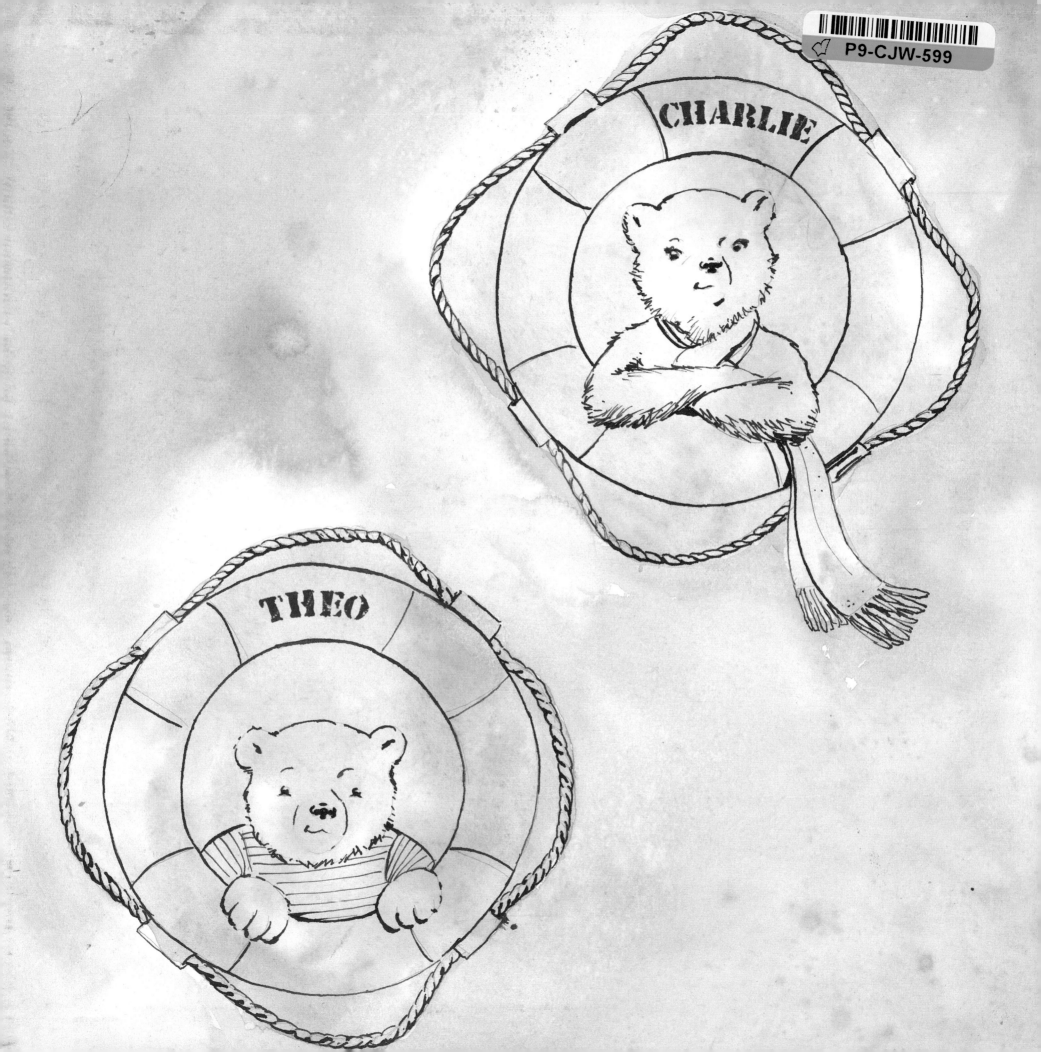

To Jacky, without whom, I'd be lost at sea

DIAL BOOKS FOR YOUNG READERS
Published by the Penguin Group • Penguin Group (USA) LLC
375 Hudson Street, New York, New York 10014

USA / Canada / UK / Ireland / Australia / New Zealand / India / South Africa / China
penguin.com
A Penguin Random House Company

Library of Congress Cataloging-in-Publication Data
Soman, David, author, illustrator.
Three bears in a boat / by David Soman.
pages   cm
Summary: Afraid to face their mother after breaking her beautiful blue seashell, three bears set out on an high seas adventure to try to find a replacement.
ISBN 978-0-8037-3993-2 (hardcover)
[1. Brothers and sister—Fiction. 2. Bears and boating—Fiction. 3. Adventure and adventurers—Fiction. 4. Bears—Fiction.] I. Title.
PZ7.S696224Thr 2014
[E]—dc23   2013017796

Manufactured in China on acid-free paper

10 9 8 7 6 5 4 3 2 1

Designed by Jasmin Rubero

Text set in Bembo Infant MT Std

Three Bears in a Boat

by DAVID SOMAN

DIAL BOOKS FOR YOUNG READERS | AN IMPRINT OF PENGUIN GROUP (USA) LLC

Once there were three bears, Dash, Charlie, and Theo, who lived by the sea.

One day, when their mother was out, the three bears
did something they really shouldn't have, and with a crash, their mother's
beautiful blue seashell lay scattered in pieces across the floor.

Afraid of their mama, who, after all, was a bear, the three fled from their house down to the beach, and huddled behind their boat.

Theo whispered nervously, "What should we do?"
Charlie just crossed her arms and stared out at the sea.
It was Dash, as usual, who had an idea. "What if we find another blue seashell, and put it back before Mama gets home? She'll never even know that anything happened."

Charlie and Theo smiled. And so just like that, the sly bears slid their boat into the sea and set sail.

Their sail flew open like a wing, and the boat flashed across the water. Dotting the sea around their home were many other bears in boats. Surely one of them would know where they could find a blue seashell.

But the bears on the first boat did not have any idea where to look.

The bears in the second boat were a little confused.

And the bears in the third boat seemed a bit busy.

Then they met a big, salty bear, and asked him if he knew where any blue seashells might be.

The salty bear looked them up and down with his keen, old sailor eyes. "I reckon I might," he said.

"A ways over yonder," he told them, "is an island shaped like a lumpy hat. On that island, there may be a seashell, a beautiful blue one. It could be underwater, or in the tallest tree, or on the very top of the mountain. It might even be hidden in a cave. I'm not dead certain, but, if you look in the right place, I reckon you'll find it."

As he began to motor away, the three little bears yelled their thanks to him. "Just look in the right place," he said with a wave of his big old paw.

Excited, and sure that they would soon have a new shell
for their mother, the three bears sailed on.

They sailed past islands that looked like a lot of fun.

And past some that maybe didn't.

Their voyage was not without incident.

They sailed on farther than they had ever gone before.

They sailed until the island rose in a hump before them, and began to search for the seashell.

They didn't find it underwater.

It wasn't in the trees.

Nor on top of the mountain.

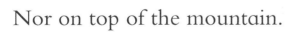

Then they found a small cave.
"I'm not going in there," squeaked Theo. "It's dark!"
"But, this *has* to be the right place," said Dash,
peering in. "We've looked everywhere else."

Then Charlie walked inside.
"Bears afraid of a cave . . ." she snorted, and the other two followed.
Inside, the cave was small and dark, and there was definitely no blue seashell.

The three were most unhappy, and stared at each other with
very squinty, very mad bear eyes, all the way back to their boat.
They had no blue seashell, and they felt very far from home.

Back on the boat, the three bears began to argue.

Dash said to Theo, "We're all stuck out here because you broke the seashell!"

And Theo yelled, "It's Charlie's fault because she was too wobbly!"

And Charlie growled, "No I wasn't! And it was Dash's idea to sneak the honey in the first place!"

And round and round they went, getting madder and madder, and louder and louder, yelling and pointing their paws at each other. They didn't even notice how the sky had been turning darker and darker, and how the sea had turned rougher and rougher until . . .

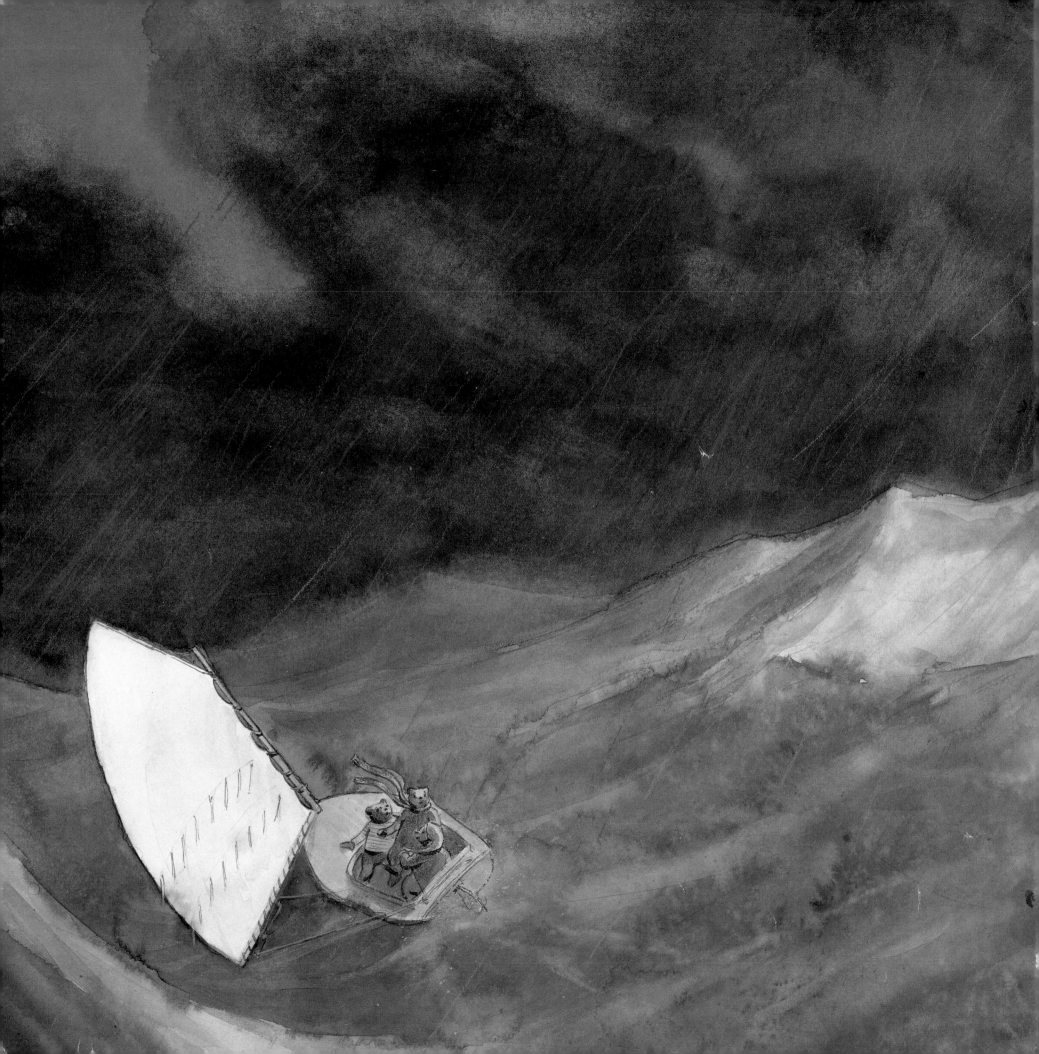

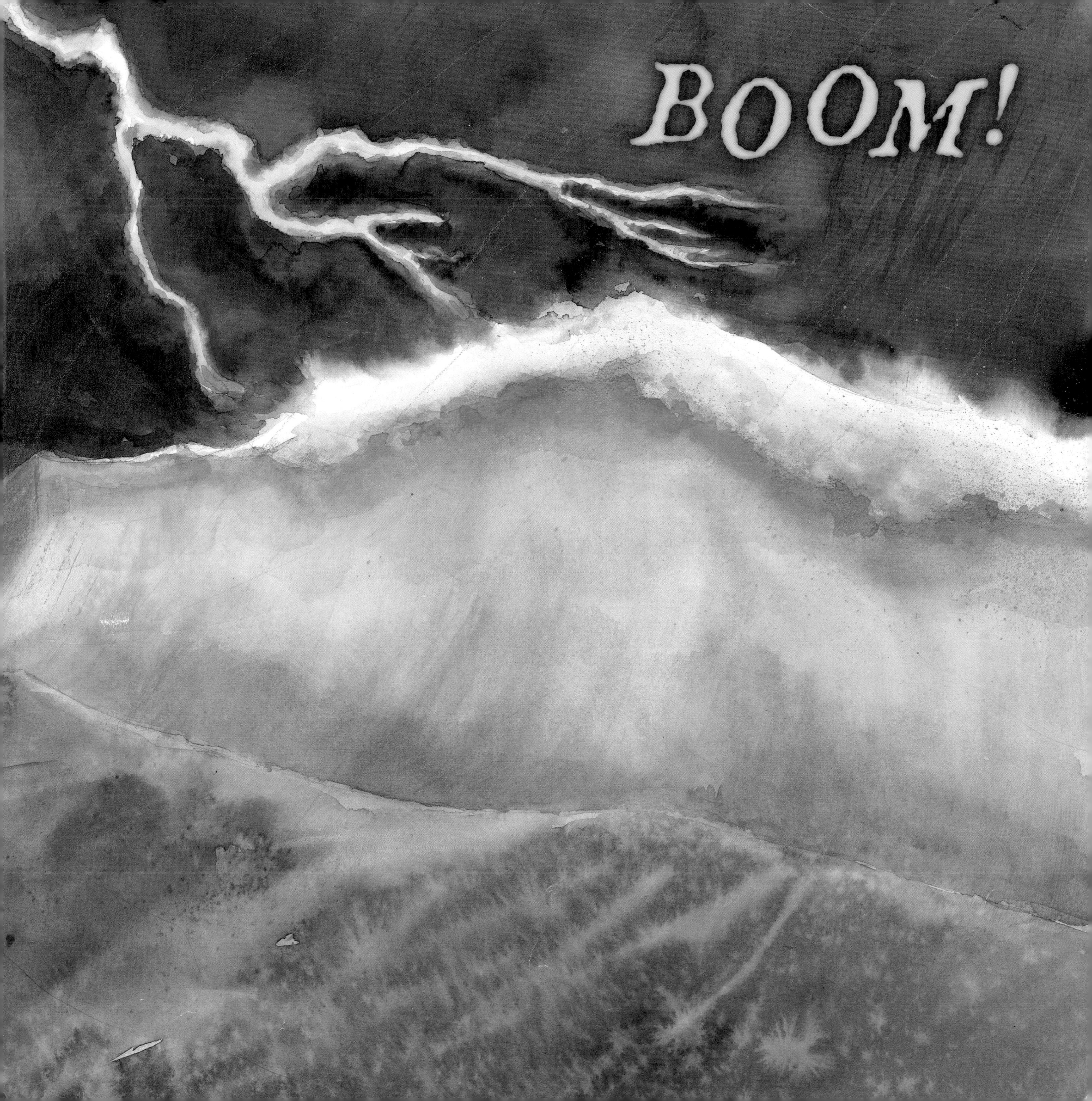
BOOM!

Dash, Charlie, and Theo were scared. They didn't care whose fault
it was anymore, they were all in the same boat.
Wet and blinking, the three bears looked at each other.
And Dash said, "It was my really bad idea."
And Theo said, "It was an accident, but I did knock the shell over."
And Charlie said, "Well, I guess I *was* sort of wobbly."
They reached out their paws and clung to each other very tightly.

And then, like turning a page, the little boat sailed out of the storm and into the sun. The three bears floated on water as smooth and calm as glass. The storm already seemed far, far behind them. And there, straight ahead, was their very own island. The bears set sail for home. They knew what they had to do.

They pulled their boat up on their own shore, and at the edge of the beach sat a beautiful blue seashell. Picking up the shell, Dash remembered the words of the old, salty bear. "So, *this* was the right place?" he asked, looking at his brother and sister.

Then the three bears walked up the long dune to their house.

Mama was waiting for them.

"I'm sorry I broke your shell," said Theo.

"Me too," said Dash.

"Me three," said Charlie.

"But look what we found for you!"

Dash held up the beautiful new shell.

And Mama Bear, being a mother, looked at each one
of her three little bears, hugged them all very, very tight,
kissed the tops of their furry heads, and forgave them.

Then she brought them inside for a warm supper.

But they didn't get any dessert.